CREEPY McPHEE

CORINNE FENTON

Illustrated by
Elizabeth Alger

SupaDOOpERS

sundance
A Haights Cross Communications Company

Published by
Sundance Publishing
P.O. Box 740
One Beeman Road
Northborough, MA 01532
800-343-8204
www.sundancepub.com

Copyright © text Corinne Fenton
Copyright © illustrations Elizabeth Alger
Project commissioned and managed by
Lorraine Bambrough-Kelly, The Writer's Style
Designed by Cath Lindsey/design rescue

First published 1999 by
Addison Wesley Longman Australia Pty Limited
95 Coventry Street
South Melbourne 3205 Australia
Exclusive United States Distribution: Sundance Publishing

ISBN 0-7608-6627-9

Contents

For Grant, Briana, and Wade, with love.

CHAPTER 1
Locked In

The door shut behind him. There was no turning back, no way to change his mind.

Lee took a few steps forward, his hands outstretched before him. A narrow ray of light trickled through a crack, high in the ceiling.

"Ouch!" His foot kicked something. Lee continued slowly, feeling his way forward in the dark.

Finally he came to another door, another handle. It creaked, as though it didn't want to be opened. But it did open, and Lee stepped through the doorway.

He found himself in a dimly lit hallway.
He heard the deadlock click behind him.
He was locked in!

Ahead he could just make out the shapes of three more doors. What would he find behind those doors? And where were those strange noises he could hear coming from?

CHAPTER 2

Watching and Wondering

Lee sighed. How had he gotten into this?
It was all Eddie's fault. It was Eddie who
first said, "Hey, Lee, look at that creepy
looking man. And what's he doing with
those boxes?"

The day had started out as a fairly ordinary one. Lee and his best friend, Eddie, were carrying out their usual Saturday morning watching-game.

Then Eddie grabbed Lee's arm. "Hey, he's coming out now," he said.

Lee and Eddie had been watching the man for several weeks. They called him Creepy McPhee.

Creepy McPhee seemed to come and go at all times of the day. Steel-rimmed glasses rested halfway down his nose, and he always looked like he slept in his clothes.

"And those boxes he carries in and out are *always* covered with dark cloths," Eddie had said.

Lee and Eddie had racked their brains about the boxes they'd seen Creepy McPhee loading in and out of his van. What was in them? What was he up to?

As they watched Creepy McPhee put the last box into his van, Eddie nudged Lee with his elbow. "Hey, look! Creepy's leaving. What would you say to doing a little snooping while he's gone? Now's our chance to peek in his windows!"

CHAPTER 3

Looking Around

As Lee and Eddie got closer to the house, they heard animal whimpers. Unsure of what to do at first, the boys decided to go see if something needed help. Noticing an open window, Lee climbed inside. But before Eddie could follow, the old window fell shut with a thump. It was stuck tight!

Lee called to Eddie through the closed window, "Eddie, wait there for me!"

Eddie was really worried! He didn't want anything bad to happen to Lee. And going into Creepy's house hadn't been planned.

Last week, Lee and Eddie had thought that Creepy McPhee was a TV or a computer thief. The boxes were the right size. But after hearing the whimpering noises, Lee knew that they'd been wrong. Creepy must be doing something to animals! Experiments that hurt them? When he found out, Eddie and he would report Creepy to the police!

Lee walked across the small, untidy bedroom, toward the door. His hands shook with fear.

There's no choice, Lee thought, as he stood in the hallway. I've just got to try *all* the doors.

He opened the first door quickly. He found himself staring into an empty cupboard!

The second door was so well locked that the doorknob wouldn't turn at all.

There was only one door left. It was at the end of the hallway. The strange noises must be coming from behind it!

Lee took a deep breath, then crept toward the door.

A tiny dot of light escaped from the keyhole. Lee screwed up one eye and peeped through.

CHAPTER 4

A Smuggler, Perhaps

This room was brightly lit. And around the edges, Lee could see rows of cages.

Lee touched the door lightly, and it opened.

He quickly walked across to the closest
row of cages. He saw that each cage was
home to some kind of animal. There were
snakes, some other reptiles, and animals of
all shapes and sizes.

One of the cages held a wise-looking turtle. Another held a sleeping opossum. Lee tickled its tail!

"Hmmm. So you're not a thief," Lee said to himself. "You're a smuggler, Creepy McPhee. An *animal* smuggler!"

Lee heard some more strange noises coming from beyond a sturdy wire gate. As he opened it, something swooped low over his head. Was it a bat? A bird? Or . . . ?

CHAPTER 5

The Mystery Deepens

Lee looked upward as birds screeched and soared around him.

There were cockatoos, small parrots, and other kinds of brightly colored birds. Some were in cages, and others were flying freely.

The whole area was covered in a type of clear dome. It wasn't a room, but rather an outside area shielded by a movable lid.

Lee heard footsteps. And they were coming toward him!

CHAPTER 6
Scared Stiff

Was it Eddie? Had he managed to open the window? No way—not by himself.

He had to hide quickly. But where? His heart thumped heavily as he squeezed behind some bird cages.

Someone came in through the door. Lee heard heavy footsteps and a dragging sound.

Then he saw Creepy McPhee. Lee had never seen him so close. He was half carrying, half dragging another large, black box.

Creepy McPhee had his back to Lee. He was so near now that Lee could smell his aftershave.

The box was very heavy. As the man wiped the sweat from his brow, his eyes glanced past the cages. Lee held his breath and stayed *so* still . . .

CHAPTER 7

Discovered!

"Hey, you! What are you doing there?"

Lee froze. Creepy McPhee seemed so angry that Lee was almost too scared to speak. Then he gazed at the enormous box.

"I know what you're up to," Lee accused. "At first, Eddie and I thought you stole TVs and computers. But now I know you're not a thief. You're an animal smuggler! You always cover those boxes so no one can see the animals you're smuggling. I'm going to tell the police."

"Quite the little detective, aren't you?" said
Creepy McPhee.

Lee made a move toward the door.

"Hold on!" Creepy McPhee said. "First of all, *I'm* the one who should call the police since you have no business being in my house! And you think I'm an animal smuggler? Well—your imagination has simply run wild!"

Creepy McPhee continued, "Now let me show you something." He pulled a business card out of his pocket.

> *Professor David Lawrence*
> Animal Protection Authority

The instant Lee read the words on the card, he realized that he'd been wrong.

"I'm a scientist. My job is to bring injured and sick animals here to take care of them. I keep them until they are fit and healthy," Professor Lawrence explained.

The Professor removed the black cover slowly and gently from the crate he had just brought in.

Inside, Lee saw a large lizard sleeping in the corner of the crate.

"So that's why you're always carrying boxes with covers on them," said Lee.

The Professor nodded. "The covers help keep the animals calm when I move them."

Sheepishly, Lee looked up and said, "I'm really sorry for everything, Professor. None of this should ever have happened."

CHAPTER 8

Another Day

"So that's the end of watching Creepy McPhee," Lee said, as he sat by the front fence with Eddie.

As they got up to go inside, Eddie glanced down the street.

"Hey, look," he exclaimed. "The new people in Number 16. Have you noticed how weird their clothes are? And the strange music that comes from their house? Lee, are you listening?"

"No way, Eddie," Lee said. *"I'm out of here!"*

Corinne Fenton

Corrine Fenton spends as much time as possible writing children's books. She also works part-time for the Children's Book Council.

Corinne gets some of her ideas for her children's books from her family. In between writing, she often spends time chasing her two pet baby goats, Sugar and Cinnamon, around the yard. Sugar and Cinnamon are supposed to eat only grass, but sometimes the young goats prefer trees and flowers.

Elizabeth Alger

 Elizabeth Alger is an illustrator of children's books, but she occasionally likes to write them as well. She lives with two cats and two ancient horses. Throughout her life she has taken in unwanted horses and given them a good home for life.

Once in a while, Liz likes to go sailing on tall ships. She has sailed across the Atlantic and Indian oceans and throughout the Bermuda Triangle on the two largest sailing ships in the world.